EMILY UMILY

Story
Kathy Corrigan

Illustrations
Vlasta van Kampen

Annick Press Ltd.,
Toronto, Canada M2N 5S3

Design and graphic realization Vlasta van Kampen

Annick Press gratefully acknowledges the contributions of
The Canada Council and The Ontario Arts Council

Canadian Cataloguing in Publication Data

Corrigan, Kathy
    Emily Umily

ISBN 0-920236-96-0 (bound) — 0-920236-99-5 (pbk.)

I. Van Kampen, Vlasta. II. Title.

PS8555.077E43 1984   jC813'.54   C84-098916-4
PZ7.C67Em 1984

Distribution in Canada and the USA by:
Firefly Books Ltd.
3520 Pharmacy Ave., Unit 1c
Scarborough, Ontario
M1W 2T8

Printed and bound in Canada by
D.W. Friesen & Sons Ltd.

Once there was a girl named Emily, aged only five. It was time for Emily to go to school, to kindergarten, but Emily didn't want to go.

"I'm only five," she told her mother, feeling quite small and not very brave at all. "And, um, I might not, um, like it there."

"We'll see dear," said her mother.

Emily went to school.

She came on the first day wearing her brand new pair of red sneakers without even one scuff on them. She met the teacher and lots of children, and the woman who gave music classes on the xylophones. Emily's mother stayed a while before going to her exercise class.

When it came time to sit on the carpet, Emily joined all the other children in a circle. She listened while a boy told about the beans he had picked in his garden and gave each kid one to eat. She listened as another boy showed the stuffed hippopotamus he had got for his birthday last week. Emily did not say anything.

Emily didn't say anything at circle time all week. A few days later the teacher said, "Well Emily, we haven't heard from you yet. What did you bring to show us?"

"Um, I um," said Emily, "I got some new, um, sneakers. Um, um, they're red."

Three children giggled. "How come you say 'um' so much?" asked one of them.

Emily's face turned as red as her sneakers. She sat very still and quiet, not looking at anybody.

"Well, they are very nice sneakers," said the teacher, trying to make Emily feel better. She didn't.

Emily tried hard to like school. Some of it was fun, like watching the guinea pigs scurry around in their cage, or playing in the sandbox, or building with the big blocks.

One day Emily painted a picture with her favourite colours, and she liked it so much she brought it in at circle time.

"I, um, I made this picture. Um, it's, um, got red in it, and um, um, and blue, and um, purple too. Um, um, and then I um, painted the black," said Emily, very proud of the colours in her painting.

None of the children were looking at the picture. They were staring at Priscilla who had been busy counting on her fingers all the time Emily had talked.

"You said 'um' nine times! I counted!" laughed Priscilla as she held up all the fingers and thumb on one hand and all the fingers on the other.

Emily's face turned as red as her painting. She sat very still and quiet, not looking at anybody.

"Well it is a very nice painting," said the teacher, trying to make Emily feel better. She didn't.

Emily still tried hard to like school. She took all the blocks and built enormous castles with thick walls and drawbridges. She made tunnels in the clay. Sometimes she sat in the book corner and read stories to herself. She was afraid to read them out loud; someone might count her um's if she did that.

Then one day Emily's big fat cat had three kittens. Emily's mother helped take all the cats to school in a bright red basket. She stayed a little while, watching the children pat the kittens, before going off to her exercise class.

At circle time the teacher asked Emily how she was going to name the kittens.

"Um," said Emily, "Um, one is Freddy, the um, white one. And um, um, the one with the um black tail is um Blackie. And, um, the other one is um, um, is Violet."

"Um, um!" cried Priscilla. "All you say is um! Your name isn't Emily. It's

UMILY!"

"Umily! Umily!" all the kids laughed. "Emily's an Umily!"

Emily's face turned as red as the kittens' basket. She sat very still and quiet, not looking at anybody.

This time the teacher didn't even bother to say that they were very nice kittens. She knew it wouldn't make Emily feel better. She was right.

Emily hated school. When she walked past their cage and the guinea pigs smiled at her, Emily didn't even smile back. She built a cave out of the big blocks and crawled in, pretending to be a bear asleep for the winter. She scratched at any kids who came near, and growled a deep growl. She didn't talk at all. Pretty soon everyone left her alone, even the teacher.

Finally the Christmas holidays came.

Instead of going to school, Emily went along to her mother's exercise class. Emily's mother pulled some mats from the pile, one for her and one for Emily. They joined in the circle with the others, each person sitting cross-legged on a mat.

"We always do this at the beginning," said Emily's mother. "You sit very still and quiet. It's called meditating."

Emily sat very still, looking out in front of her, not really thinking about anything at all. The only sound was that of her own breathing, quietly in and out, getting softer and softer.

After what seemed like a very long time, the teacher said, "Now while you are sitting like that, we are going to try something new. We are going to chant."

She showed all the people how to sit with their legs crossed and their backs straight, and how to make their thumbs and first fingers into little round o's resting on their knees.

Then the teacher breathed in a long breath. As she let the breath slowly out of her mouth, a word came with it. "UMMM," she said. "UMMMMM," loud and deep and clear. The um rumbled out right from down in her belly. It went on and on until all of her breath was gone. Then she took another breath and began to chant again.

"UMMMMMMMMMMMMMMMMMMMMMMMMMM . . ."

"Oh!" thought Emily. "Oh yes!" It was the best sound she had ever heard in her whole life, even if she was only five.

On the first day back at school Emily didn't say a word all morning. She waited until it was circle time and the children were sitting together on the floor. Then, before the teacher could ask who had something new today, Emily spoke:

"Um, I um, I want to show you what I learned on vacation."

Everyone was so surprised to hear Emily talk again that they forgot to count her ums.

"Um, it's um, it's a chant. Um, um . . . .". Emily showed them how to sit cross-legged with their thumbs and first fingers making little round o's on their knees. She told them how to take a deep breath and how to let out the um sound slow and rumbly.

When Emily nodded they all took a deep breath. Together they began to chant "UMMMMMMMMM" until, one by one, they ran out of breath. And when all the other children had stopped, Emily was still chanting UMMMM even though her face was turning red.

"Well that is a very nice chant," said the teacher. "And Emily, you do it so well."

"Yes," said Emily smiling. "Um, I, um, I've had a lot of um, practice."

Everyone laughed, even Emily.

The, um, End.